T0142699

The story of Mr. Sandman

BETH PHILLIPS

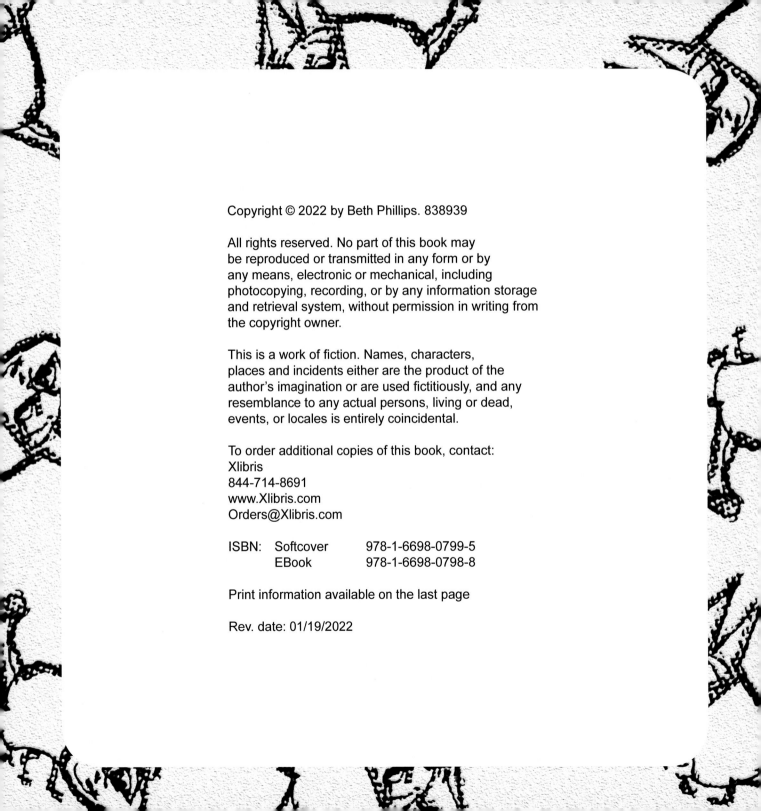

To order additional copies of this book, contact:
Xlibris
844-714-8691
www.Xlibris.com
Orders@Xlibris.com

ISBN: Softcover   978-1-6698-0799-5
        EBook   978-1-6698-0798-8

Print information available on the last page

Rev. date: 01/19/2022

This book belongs to:

Grateful acknowledgements:

Pet Resource Center of Hillsborough County Animal service aka Pet Resource Center.

I went to the shelter to adopt a cat I had my eye on. When I got there the cat was gone. The volunteer said take this one. I said what is that one? She said Sandman. I said "what is that?" She sang "Mr. Sandman sing me a song."

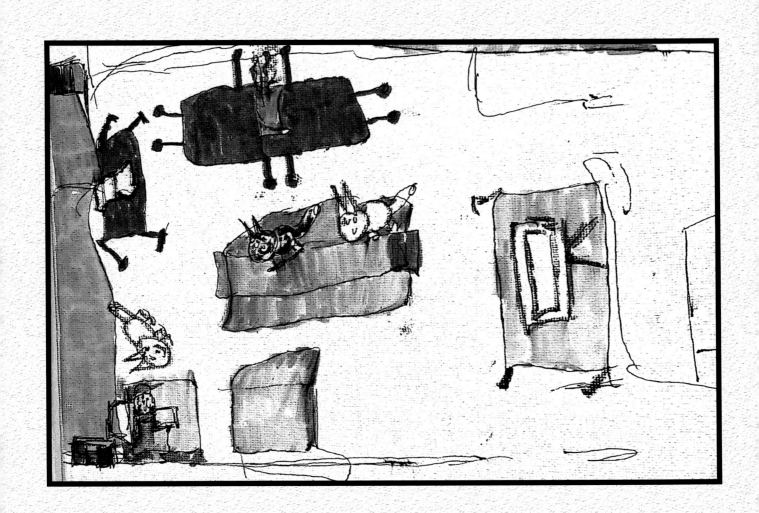

Mr. Sandman went to live in his new home. A one bedroom apartment with his new friends. Those being Zoe and Dhali. A generous person offered to put up a fence for them.

Within a year they moved to a new home. Mr. Sandman liked to hang out in the loft room. Zoe spent hours each day running up the staircase to the loft and jumping down to the cat tower.

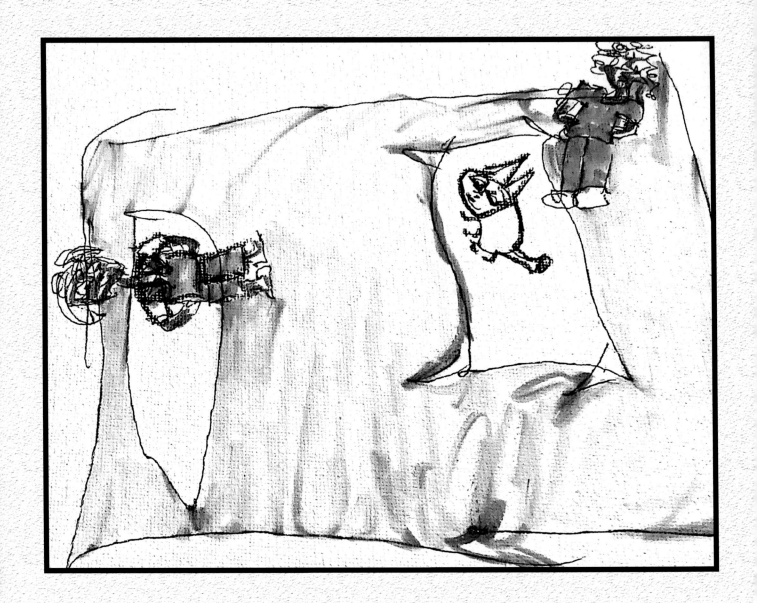

Sadly, Dhali got sick and was diagnosed with congestive heart failure.

Mr Sandman likes playing the piano and composes too.

Mr. Sandman loves all the pets and greets them. Mr. Sandman was very fond of Shelby.

Mr. Sandman and Zoe became the best of friends.

During the day Zoe walks around the neighborhood while Mr. Sandman rolls around at the edge of the driveway.

In 2017, Mr. Sandman went on a vacation to the Lakeshore Villas where he met Brownie the Streetcat and beyond.

But after several break ins and a very pushy man Mr. Sandman returned back to his house. Sadly, Brownie was left behind as the owner of the house Mr. Sandman returned to did not want another cat. Fortunately, a nice couple took Brownie in. It was very interesting how Brownie had traveled over 20 miles from the home he was adopted into to be an outdoor working cat to the Lakeshore Villa housing development.

In the summer of 2021 Mr. Sandman got two new family members. Chip and Dale. Two winter white hamsters. Fourth of July was a blast. There were sparklers and everyone had fun.

Shortly after... sadly one of the hamsters disappeared. Great efforts were taken to locate the hamster. Not by their veterinarian but by others that cared. Being that he couldn't have gotten out of his main habitat by himself PETA investigated. PETA said I tried to get an autopsy but was given the run around. Sadly, the second hamster was found transitioned to the next life back in one of his many habitats. Being unable to break the news to their fan club the kid's tennis camp I continued to report that everything was okay. After a retaliation where I was subjected to yelling "Peter doesn't want you there!!", the break ins, the local tennis store pretending not to get my money and asking questions being told "I don't know." I finally lost my temper pushed belongings off a dresser and sprayed my husband with a water hose. The police were called and with a serious back injury I was put on the ground and held down by two police officers with their knees in my badly injured back and then handcuffed and taken to Gracepoint where I spent two days.

The end for now.